Two Hoots

Helen Cresswell
and
Colin West

Young Lions

Published in Young Lions 1988
Fourth impression March 1990

Young Lions is an imprint of
the Children's Division, part of
the Collins Publishing Group,
8 Grafton Street, London W1X 3LA

Printed and bound in Great Britain by
William Collins Sons & Co. Ltd, Glasgow

There were these two owls who
lived in Shooters Wood.

The rest of the owls called them
the Two Hoots.

Not this pair. The Two Hoots were as daft as coots. Nobody knew how they got like that, not even the wise owls. From the moment they hatched they were daft.

Oooh— look at that!

It's a big fat white bird with no beak and no claws!

The Two Hoots were not only daft,
they didn't know day from night.

They went flapping round the wood
all day long while the other owls
were asleep.

The trouble was that when the sun was shining, the Two Hoots couldn't see very well.

The Two Hoots could hardly see
past their own beaks.

The wise owls got very fed up with this, so one night they held a big meeting. They thought that the Two Hoots were fast asleep.

Boss Owl sat on a stump and the rest flew down around him.

They didn't see the Two Hoots, who were awake for once.

12

So a list was drawn up.

RULES FOR WISE OWLS

1 All owls to be wise at all times.

2 No flying around between Sunrise and Sunset.

3 Any owl caught not obeying Rules 1 and 2, to be thrown out of Shooters Wood.

(signed)

Boss Owl

INK

The notice was pinned to the tree
where the Two Hoots lived.

Then the rest of the owls flew off
to catch mice.

The Two Hoots waited till they'd
gone, then flew back to their hole.

Big Hoot read out the rules to Little
Hoot, who wasn't too hot at reading.

LATER . . .
Class 4 of Witherspoon Road Junior
School were piling out of the coach
that had drawn up to Shooters Wood.

Their teacher, Miss Toasty (who was really crummy) had brought them on a nature ramble.

18

19

Billy Mayne meant to catch a dragon. With any luck, it would breathe fire.

Susie Potts wanted to find a witch. She wasn't too sure she believed in them, but wanted to find one anyway.

Abdul Singh was very keen on catching a crocodile.

Miss Toasty would have had a fit if she had been a mind reader.

Bless their little hearts!

George and Julie Boot had their
own plans, which had nothing at all
to do with a nature ramble.

MEANWHILE . . .
The Two Hoots knew nothing about
the arrival of Class 4 of Witherspoon
Road Junior School.

They perched glumly outside their hole.

Little Hoot waved his
wing toward the notice.

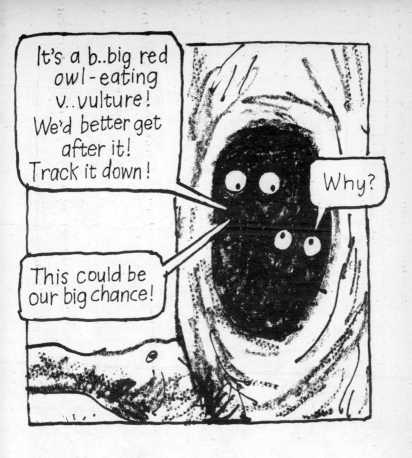

The Two Hoots clean forgot about
Rule 2.

2 No flying around
between Sunrise
and Sunset.

They took off after the red vulture. It came down with a

WHOOOOSH

and perched in a high tree.

The Two Hoots slammed on their brakes.

'I've had a wise thought!' said Little
Hoot. 'We mustn't let it see us!'
'Good thinking!' Big Hoot told him.
'I've had an even wiser thought!
Let's fly back and warn the others!'
'That's it! We'll save their lives!
We'll be heroes!'

Back they flew, hooting like mad.

31

It was beginning to look as if it didn't pay to be wise. In the end Boss Owl said he'd go and take a look.

He was back in less than no time.

MEANWHILE . . .
quite nearby in Shooters Wood,
Class 4 of the Witherspoon Road
Junior School were getting peckish.
Miss Toasty clapped her hands.

> Here, children! Bring your
> specimens and note books.

1 creepy crawly
in net
(to put in
sister's bed)

1 handful
of stones
(to be used
in caterpult)

1 caterpillar
in jar
(to put in best
friend's lettuce)

1 leaf with
cuckoo spit
(because it looks
revolting)

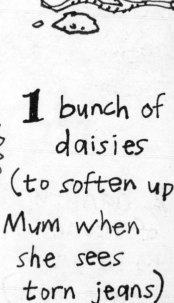

1 bunch of
daisies
(to soften up
Mum when
she sees
torn jeans)

Billy Mayne, Susie Potts and Abdul
Singh said that their specimens
were too big to put in jars.
'We just made notes and drawings,'
they told Miss Toasty.

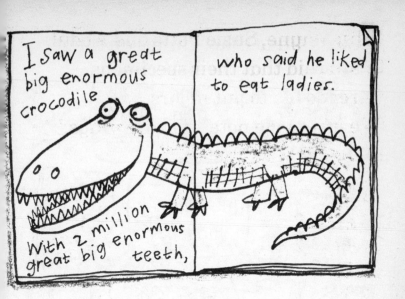

Class 4 had other things on their minds.

Class 4 scrambled.

They had their lunch boxes open in a flash and were soon scoffing

crisps,

sausages,

egg and cress sandwiches,

chocolate,

lettuce,

sticky buns, celery, cheese rolls, crispbread and apples.

There was silence but for the munching of Class 4 Witherspoon Road Junior School.

WHOOOOO! WHIT TOWHOOOO!

Miss Toasty choked on her nut cutlet.

This is amazing! This is a new breed of owl! We must find it! Oh – it will be in all the textbooks!

THINKS:

TOASTY OWL

TOASTY OWL
A very rare breed discovered by Miss E. Toasty in Shooters Wood in 1985

Class 4 went on munching.

There will be a prize for whoever spots it first!

Class 4 moved like greased lightning.

The Two Hoots watched them go.
They were very fond of crisps,

sausages, egg and cress sandwiches

sticky buns, and apple pie . . .

They stuffed themselves so full
they could hardly fly.

Then Class 4 came puffing back
from their wild goose chase
(or wild owl chase).

AND THEN . . .

THE GREATEST MOMENT OF Miss Toasty's Life...

Miss Toasty sprinted off.
Class 4 of Witherspoon Road Junior
School trailed after her.

TWO HOURS LATER . . .
In Shooters Wood silence reigned.
Even the Two Hoots were fast
asleep, podged by their picnic.

A van drew up
at the edge
of the
wood.

hen another van.
he wood was being invaded.

A TV crew had arrived!

MEANWHILE . . .
The Two Hoots were just waking
from their nap. Almost at once they
remembered that today they must
leave Shooters Wood forever.

The TV crew froze.

They crashed into the clearing where
the owls lived.
The sparks connected the lights.

Our heroes were blinded
by the dazzle.

The sound man pushed his boom up through the leaves.

The interviewer was so excited that he could hardly speak.

Here we are in Wooters Shood — I mean Shooters Wood, in broad daylight! And there — as you can see — are what are certain almostly — I mean almost certainly — the only pair of a rare breed of owls in England today...

TOASTY OWLS!

shrieked Miss Toasty hysterically.

The light and the racket woke all the other owls.

You may have seen the programme
yourself.

The Two Hoots became
famous overnight.

Shooters Wood was made into an
Owl Sanctuary.

Ornithologists came from all over the
world to spot the famous Toasty Owls.

And by now there were
dozens of Toasty Owls.

All the owls wanted to be famous.
Even Boss Owl gave up hunting at
night and became a daylight owl.

Except that he wasn't Boss Owl
any more.

The Two Hoots turned out to be not
so daft, after all!